# THE TALES of
# RON-SAN
## Or An
## AMERICAN
# NAGOYA

By

Michael Yarbrough

The Tales of Ron-San or an American in Nagoya

**Copyright © Michael Yarbrough 2022**

**BantamWings Publishing**
**167 Madison Avenue Suite 205**
**New York, NY 10016**
**www.bantamwings.com**

**ISBN 978-1-958126-11-0**

Printed in the United States of America

# CONTENTS

# PROLOGUE

Nagoya is divided into three parts. (If the style is the man, let the reader note this as the style of one who can cope.) There is first of all the city's most delightful aspect, that small part surviving American bombers and Japanese post-war developers that evokes traditional Japan. Its few temples of note include one of Japan's principal Shinto shrines, Asuta Jingu.

In districts otherwise not at all notable, one can find such islands of wonder as original illustrative scrolls for what may be the greatest work of Japanese literature, The Tale of Genji, this in the Nagoya Museum of Fine Arts. Another is Tsuruma Park, more to my taste than the Luxembourg of Paris.

The second part is the new city, a functionalist phantasm. A foreigner will find its rents and prices overall the most reasonable of any major city in Japan. A subway system that is clean, safe, efficient and rapid will take you almost anywhere in the city. Some kinds of work for foreigners such as teaching are more available than in most other places.

If this second part bores you as it does me to write about it, its third part may interest you more. Some think I am its most original denizen, so my guidance may please you.

# The Artist
## of the SHADOWS

**H**ow might such a place have looked before the war?" I wondered not for the first time as I sat, imbibing a mizuwari, and looking on from the table I had chosen in a dark corner. The interior I did not regard as particularly Japanese: white walls framed with dark, heavy beams. The pictures gracing them were, as to be expected, those of post-war artists, all of them, except for one, by a Japanese. I could be corrected – again, not for the first time – that before the war, such places were not tolerated.

"Rot!" I reflected with a fondly received Britishism, "Where there's a will and enough money, there's a way."

"Ron-san?" a voice behind me asked in English, "Would you like another?"

"No, I wouldn't, Yoshiaki," I said, turning, "but how are you this evening? Long time no see...No, don't look at me like that. I was here just long enough to teach you that one. Hisashiburi ne."

"Yes. Yes, that's true," he said in an uncertain English, and then in Japanese, added, "But you weren't here for very long. You left very suddenly, and I didn't expect to see you again. Are you working here tonight?"

His laughing eyes and smile, I took in with humor; his youth and good looks, with jealous admiration. Many times, I had thought, "What my life would have been like had I looked like him!" I only replied, "I'm here by special arrangement with Keiko. Just seeing a friend. You may not have seen her here for a long while either. I'm paying for the evening –"

"You're kidding!" he laughed, "No, you're crazy! No wonder you left suddenly. Oh well, you were our only painter. There it is. Keiko won't let Hiro take it down."

"Yes, it's too bad more people don't appreciate some of the finer things in life," I said, smiling as I brought the drink to my lips.

"The finer things in life! You, Ron-san!" he said, laughing as he moved away before adding in English, "See you later, alligator!"

Hmmm. I wondered if my "friend" would agree enough with him or with me, too, perhaps to actually make her way to this absurd tryst. When we had last met, she had not had so much as a chance to know she should have a choice. And money? We might as well have met in a park. It was fate that brought us together, as they say (much too often). That's hardly the cliche to compel further reading, I know, Dear Reader – nineteenth-century this time – but, as you'll see, if you dare, I don't need you to pay the rent. In any case, what else can you call whatever accounts for two people from assuredly different walks of life and of only the briefest previous acquaintance being seated together on an expensive airplane?

I recognized her at once, and was gleeful with her failure to recognize me. I know that she mistook that glee for the fervor of an artist setting to work...but, then...I have the vanity to think that in a way, she was right.

I like to use pastels on the plane. They don't drip. In any case, at the higher altitudes, the colors and contours below all fade, the forms passing so quickly that you can only draw whatever lasting fantasies they evoke.

She didn't take long to note over my shoulder the incongruity of the ground below with my sketch.

"Excuse me, sir, do you speak Japanese?" she began in English.

I replied affirmatively in Japanese. I have a fine memory for appearances, as the reader shall see, and not only with the eye of an artist. Still, she was not young and beautiful, if that's what you think. No, she was middle-aged and beautiful. I knew her to be forty-six. I remember liking her taste in clothes before: with simplicity of cut, always, I suspect, like a good, modern Japanese, but at least away from her own people, with the elegance of her own taste, a discerning preciosity.

"It's unusual for people to bring pastels onto a plane, isn't it? But still, it's a nice thing to see." Such a lovely, oval face!

"Yes, I'm not really very good," I said with a false modesty I put on when speaking to Japanese. (And which they love, even the many who feel that I have little to be falsely modest about.)

"Well, no, you need a model for that, don't you? And a studio? Or a settled place on a mountain top?" As she spoke, I searched that intoning face; she spoke too off-handedly to be volunteering herself, I decided.

But I had not asked. The asking need not begin with a question. Alone, my interest would have been art; now, it was not. I decided I would content myself with quickly reproducing from memory the setting not of a drawing, but of a painting done about five years ago. It was set in a beachside garden in Sydney, the flight's point of origin. Not surprisingly, I began to vindicate my displeasure with the original. The stalks and boughs that would cradle her, I would make vivid and strong. The flowers that should ornament her still naturally black hair would thrust from three pots on the ground and from a faded white trestle I thought I could unobtrusively insert. But even to produce an altered copy takes time. I thought I would here sketch the outlines, then color in only the foreground framing her body. The rest I might complete later. These were my thoughts when I replied, "I have a settled place on this plane. Imagine if there were angels seated on these clouds. In this age, even if we weren't moving, it would be difficult to make more of them than a family portrait."

She laughed. "A family portrait! Yes, that's what the old European painters often did with them –"

"I didn't mean a family of daimyo," I said gently.

"Daimyo? Do you read Japanese history?"

"Oh, some things. It interests me, and I live and work in Japan. But I don't know much about Australia. Just why did you go there? Do you like Sydney?"

"Sydney? Yes, I like it. It's a beautiful place. But I was there mostly for business. I import women's clothing and household items," she said quickly. After a pause, she asked, "What did you think of it? You aren't Australian."

"No, I'm an American. I liked Sydney. It is beautiful, but I think it's like most American cities. You don't visit it just to look at historical things. You go there to look at it, and live its life for a while."

"Yes. I think so, too. But I'm an old-fashioned Japanese. I want to live in an Asian city."

"Old fashioned? You don't mean Meiji, do you? Those Japanese preferred Western things, didn't they? You mean you want old historical things to dream with, am I right?"

"Yes, that's right," she replied with a grand smile, "And you?"

"Maybe the same." I knew now which of my old Far Eastern paintings to scotch the Sydney one for. But why not simply let the conversation continue, reserving the art gambit only to fill the silence? I suddenly wanted a drink, and I beckoned to a passing stewardess. I ordered scotch and water. The woman declined to join me, but gave me her business card and name, which, to my relief, confirmed the one I remembered.

"So, Sachiko, you live in Nagoya. So, do I. Perhaps I'll see you there sometime."

"Well, come to my shop...sometime...sometime. Bring your wife, too, if you have one."

"A wife? Yes, a marriage of convenience, you could say."

"Oh, really? Most foreigners don't believe in marriages of convenience. It wasn't arranged, was it?"

"Only by us."

"Oh, I see," said Sachiko, aglow, "But what do you do?"

"I'm an English teacher."

"Oh, I see. Where?"

"Anywhere. It's the convenience afforded by a spouse's visa. Right now, she's in San Francisco, enjoying the convenience of access afforded by marriage to an American."

"I see. Very good." Her high, carved cheeks were so lovely when brightly lit.

Now would be a good time to paint, I decided. "So, tell me where you would live, if not in Nagoya?"

"Oh, if not in Nagoya? Kyoto. And probably outside of it."

I had not paintings set in Kyoto. Perhaps, it was the city's size. I did have one set in Takayama. I had sketched in most of the design on my third visit, when I had rather quickly found myself surfeited on the sights.

But why not? There was probably more of old Kyoto in Takayama than in Kyoto itself. With a demure smile, I excused myself, "Let me see if I can guess your mind."

Quickly completing the lines of a temple garden, and the figure of a woman in a kimono standing over a pool, I looked up at her directly, pointing to the still empty visage to ask, "May I?"

"So, you do need a model, do you?"

"Kind of...I don't expect you to pose rigidly. Not at all. I need to see your face..."

She laughed, leaning over to examine the figure that was to be hers. "Yes, it's a good likeness. The face is all right, but the figure is better. Much better. I would have expected it otherwise. But you're just starting on the face, and I know that faces are the hardest part."

I'm well practiced in concealing my amusement (and not only my amusement), but how could she not have begun to search herself for the source of such provocative foreknowledge? Of course, faces, even distant ones, are the hardest part, and I had only begun, but I was certain that I had rendered her form well enough to hint at confession. I was delighted when after what seemed a half-minute, she declared with a knowing nod, "Yes, the body is just right. I don't know how you could do it. Of course, please put my face in your drawing."

For the rest of the flight, we alternated between conversation and silence, while I sketched. At length, she dozed. Now, I would take a most pleasant liberty. I put aside the Takayama sketch, content with the face for now, and with my memory for later... and not only with memory. I began another study of that face, this one framed not by a reproduced painting, but a rendition of a remembered work place: white walls and heavy, dark beams. I regretted that I could not with truth make vivid the painting against the far wall, my own of Keiko.

Sachiko slept in peace, but not in the bliss that was almost the blaze I wished to make it in the painting. How could I then...? Across a table of a homey sort flushed by sun light through a bay window (which, like the table, was never to be found there), my Sachiko stretched her arms cat-like in a yawn. Myself I painted from the back, stiff and faceless, almost a silhouette; she might have been conversing rapturously with the Sphinx. I colored in the interior as much as it pleased me for the moment, enough to recall the design to me later, and to her when she awoke. I put it aside, and taking a fresh leaf, began sketching in pencil her face both as it was and as I would have it. I was still sketching when she awoke.

7

Only momentarily did her waking suggest that brilliance I would capture.

"I do wish you had been longer about that yawn. It's bad enough doing without much direct sun light in here," I said.

"What! Why?" she asked, smiling with surprise.

I showed her my progress on the drawing, then the pencil sketches. "The faces are the hardest part. I don't think you could model for this expression if you tried. Only the Pygmalion method will do here, I think."

She shook her lovely head in, I think, delighted confusion.

"Pygmalion method? That's Greek to you, is it? It is to a lot of people." Naturally, I never intended for her to understand. I was content, and made her content with an explanation of Pygmalion... the remainder of our journey being passed, as you may guess, in like banter, like scratches, and like indulgence. Dear Reader, knowing where you stand with me, you may place the passing of my phone number in whichever of these categories you like. (Yes, I drink while I write, but so did Hemingway, I think.)

As you would expect, her voice thickened upon hearing the name and address of the place. I had not chosen it out of humor alone: why shouldn't we begin again at the beginning? I explained that she would not be paying for the evening (or rather the morning), that it would be only dinner and conversation, and, lastly, that this time I would be present only as a club guest like herself.

"Like myself?" she teased, "Like no other guest, I think!" She explained that she would need about a week-and-a-half to get away from her family for an all-night rendezvous. "My husband? Oh, he'll be no problem. Discretion without questions. That's our way."

"A marriage of convenience like my own, perhaps?" I suggested.

"It is now. See you then. Bye-bye."

It was about 2:00 a.m.; she was to have been here a half-hour ago. Probably simply late. Or perhaps she was testing my ardor or my inclination to drink. But at last, after how many reflections about what – my third mizuwari – I beheld her at the door. What a glittering gown!

"One would think you were the affluent whore here!" I forbore from saying as she sat down. "How difficult it is…," I began, continuing after only the sparest pause with "not to remember the world outside as a cage right now…" in place of "to remember your age right now!" Only in part was it mizuwari and a fumbling art: I think I meant it.

The courses were shabu shabu, sashimi, a cheese and vegetable salad, and sake; the little wine we drank was ordered by the glass. All of this was possible through a special arrangement with the owner's wife, Keiko, which cost me far more than it would elsewhere and was prepared and delivered by a nearby restaurant. Early in the meal, I ordered coffee. I intended for us to talk.

Japanese small talk is often micro-talk. She had come for more than that. "I asked you here out of curiosity," I began, "What's most immediately curious is why you came…not only tonight, but the first time. This place is in your own city. You don't worry about blackmail?"

She smiled a quiet courage, then said, "The next time he comes, ask for some strong coffee in a pitcher, please…" Then looking me in the eye, as a woman from Tokyo might, she said, "I gave you my business card on the plane. I never would have here. I don't think you will blackmail me, or you wouldn't have invited me here like this, but what about you? Why this life? If it's for the money, why spare me? If not for that, then for what?" I saw only harried bewilderment.

9

I threw my head back, lifting as I did a full glass of Chianti, and quaffed it. Setting it down, I asked with a smile, "In my country, what I do with women for money is illegal; it is a crime. But is money all crime has to offer? That is no more true than to say that the police hunt down criminals only as a job or out of duty. The people you see running into each other in the same dark places when they could usually be elsewhere have more in common than most of them would admit...It's not only cynicism or despair with idealism, or even only greed that accounts for so many cops going over to the other side. It can be a personal liking."

I searched her disbelieving face. "You didn't always come to places like this, did you? You're a reluctant adventuress...It's only a recently acquired taste. Too many of you women of the older generation got married too young. You were denied your youth. Now, in your forties, some of you are having it...one way or the other..."

"How old are you?" she asked slowly, but seeming to be at last enjoying her disbelief.

"Thirty-four."

"Thirty-four? I haven't been around as much as you think. But don't younger men usually do this?"

The question was put softly enough, and I could see that she was savoring it. So was I...also my answer, "Younger men don't usually talk better, but, as you must have found, they certainly bring more to their work."

She slapped her knee – not mine – with a deep titter. She liked this kind of talk. Good. I would spice it up with more American directness, "Well, my dear Sachiko, our first time was brief, but I tried."

She was silent for a time, looking into herself more than at me; I signaled to the waiter. Then she said, "You tried very hard. Your spirit is ...very..."

"Willing," I offered, "but the flesh is weak." I received her ignorant yes-yes nod as proof of her Buddhism, and simply asked her upon the waiter's arrival, "Chardonnay? A bottle?" I conveyed her affirmative reply to the waiter, and asked her, "Sachiko, what is this life of yours, if I may ask?"

"Well, I've told you, haven't I?"

"You haven't told me if your husband would be surprised to see you in this place."

"Oh, I don't know," she said, looking up at me with mischievous glee.

"You don't know, Sachiko, and I believe you, but would the Sachiko of ten years ago be surprised at seeing you here?"

"Yes, she would...but not completely. She already knew that her husband was doing it. So did her sons. They don't hate him, because I have tried to make them understand."

"To understand? To understand what?" I asked, tapping my glass.

"That eventually it will be difficult for them not to be the same way...as I am now." She smiled her toughness.

"Are you the same?"

She smiled once more. "I'm at least the same in understanding, I hope. My husband is a good man. He helps me with business. I import, I told you. He imports liquors. He travels. I travel. A couple of Marco Polos. I have my life and my friends. He has his. I would hope my sons were as understanding. What about you?"

"What about me?"

"What are you going to do with yourself? This is no life for a man! Not a man, who is a man, such as you!"

How many times had I had this conversation! "This may be no life for a man, but it is interesting for us as well as for you, the worthy public, if done in moderate doses –"

"Moderate?"

"Moderate, yes. I rarely am with anyone I detest; I'm not into the fag trade, though I take a request as a compliment. I don't do it all the time, and I'm always quitting and working elsewhere. You don't have to be moral to know that too much of this is bad for your spirit and senses. Too much of it is bad for painting. Meanwhile, I invest, and since, as you know, respectability is largely a matter of appearances, I expect to be a solid pillar of the community before I'm forty."

"Don't you want marriage or children? Or family?" I had struck truly; where there had been toughness, there was only dismay. It was looking a long way back, but she should have been my mother.

"If I did, I would be in America having them, I suppose. Except when I teach English or paint, I'm an unconstructive...well, Marco Polo, if you will. The shadows fascinate me, and so does the light they beautify."

"So, what am I?" she asked with an amused shake of her head.

"You're what you've made of yourself from the wreckage. You didn't go to school or get married to do this. But here it is. So are you learning anything? Is it interesting? Do you think you are constructive?"

"Yes," she said with a forthright nod, "This evening with you may turn out to be, but usually no. I haven't done it for a while. I like money and sex, but I like personality as well. I should tell you that. Oh, for your last question. I'm constructive in my work, and in raising my sons. Otherwise? No."

"Would you like to be? Sachiko, would you be my model? We might become friends. I'll show you my paintings first, of course." I doubted I would ever see her again.

She laughed. Such a lovely, hearty laugh. I looked out over the table. So much talking. So little eating. So much cold food. Such a vital, warm woman.

She was looking at me with thoughtful nods while her eyes still laughed. Finally, she said, "Let me see your paintings first. If I like them, maybe I will...You'll let me get into trim first, won't you? I have my pride." To my nod, she replied, "Maybe, I'll fall in love with you, and leave sons and husband for you, and we'll sail far away."

"You'll do no such thing, Sachiko," I said, lifting the bottle, "You'll have some Chardonnay, instead."

# ChassisOrange

W hat a lady! Is that new? But no, Dear, it's you who are new!" said Ron. "I'd love to paint you in it! That spatter of white and blue and violet and...beautiful Sachiko!"

"Hanae Mori. 1968. Most people don't remember it. Keep old clothes long enough and they may become new. This shawl I bought later."

"Silk, isn't it?" Sachiko nodded. "Don't ask me about my suit. I'm a poor match."

"It's better that you not match me. People can see the age difference. Anyway, you do have your camera, don't you? Maybe you'll have time to sketch me."

"Our usual game. It does look better."

"And you like to draw!"

"I do like to draw! And I do like to have an excuse to fix on your beauty even in public. But I'll also have to alter the ambience to better frame you."

"Do! But I thought this place would be nice. Not so popular, not so crowded with noisy people, but attractive."

"The tables are nice, but the walls and wooden counters should feature paintings and maybe flowers. Not too lush. White irises, camellias, violets, pale pink roses."

"Paint them in. And remember: Not too lush!" concluded Sachiko with a smile.

It was time to change the subject. Let her do it.

"Did you meet anyone unusual at work – that you can share with me!"

A very young waitress with a perky smile came up with our drinks and tofu steaks. Sachiko was given a chassis grape a beautiful red drink with blackcurrent fruit. I took sake with this seafood concoction that I've seen sold in the basement of Matsuzakaya Department Store (Japanese Niemann-Marcus). We'd follow it with matcha ice cream.

Sachiko's timing was perfect. Now then to relate it as I later would for Aoi.

-*-

We were still lining up when I was summoned. A first-time customer had refused "the menu" – the list of hosts given to every patroness – and asked for the painter of the one wall canvas by me. I was directed to a corner table and told that tonight would be different: Normally, a new

15

patroness is visited by different hosts who share the bottle, compelling her to buy more. (Ugly? Yes, and unhealthy in every sense – but it can lead to better things!) After a conference with the manager (not Aoi's father) and a payment of 50,000 yen, the woman, one Naoko, and her friend, a 23-year-old blonde, blue-eyed American, Marla, were given a table with one seat on the aisle to the door.

Naoko was a beautiful 40, with piercing eyes, the wife of an executive for Nihon Gaishi. She had had to return with Marla to retrieve from her car items that she kept always close at hand: large tablets of heavy paper for drawing, brushes and two sets of paints and ink as well as fabrics to drape over the table and place below and beside us on the table.

She took the inside of the table, placing me by the aisle. Marla she stood by a large potted fern between ourselves and the aisle. Out of her bag, she plucked a Polaroid Instant camera with a large flash, and alternated between giving directions and snapping pictures. She then handed me the camera, "Your turn! Marla, be patient! I'll let you sit in a minute!" While I took the camera, studying the buttons, she placed the tablet and paint and ink set beside me. She then gave me a cursory explanation of the camera's workings. In effective English!

At the moment, a host strode up quickly telling us in Japanese that we couldn't do this.

Naoko looked down the aisle and across at a bar until she caught sight of the manager, and with a frown, raised her hand to stiffly signal a summons. "Not enough?" asked Naoko.

She jabbed a hand into her purse for her wallet, then opening it, briskly flipped out 3 10,000-yen notes. "Enough? Let's make the 3 into 15!" She jabbed a hand into her purse for her wallet, then opening it, briskly flipped out 15 10,000 yen notes. (Each of these about 65USD!) "Enough?" The manager, open-mouthed, then at length nodded. He, too, had probably never seen this. "Probably a woman of inherited privilege!" I thought, a type I had only read about. But why argue with John Lennon who had found his own a lot of fun?

"Do you have a cocktail menu?"

"Hai, so desu!"

Looking at me, "Chassis orange?"

"Hai, so desu," I cooed much amused. I smiled at the manager, Yoshio. His stern mien broke into a grin. "Mochiron! [Of course].

He gazed at one of the hosts with a light clap of his hands, "Chassis Orange mittsu!" "Have a good evening!" he said, looking back as he turned away. We would be left alone by all but the curious among the guests and their shimei or favorite hosts.

At length, when we had both photographed her in a variety of poses, and placed the pictures before us, Naoko directed Marla to take a seat. "I'm sorry Marla. I'm the teacher now, but here is your drink."

"And we've already eaten. I can see why."

I thought that Marla must feel greatly put upon, so I asked if she would be free for more sessions away from the club. She would be fed and paid per hour what she charged for lessons, 50.00USD. She insisted on late mornings Sunday or Tuesday, and so we exchanged phone numbers (mine for a second phone in the house dedicated to my business).

"Naoko, and you Marla, please call for anything. And, Naoko, I do want to see your work."

"You shall, Ron, but always bring what I've given you tonight!"

"Thank you, Naoko. Thank you very much. I shall."

_*_

"Marla, what did you do in America? I'm sorry I didn't ask the other night. It was Naoko's evening. She wrote our parts. We're on our own now." I sighed.

Marla was a pretty blonde. I won't detail that. After all, as I was painting, I sought to capture detail, but could not complete them without inventing more. But I was glad to be talking to another American, another night crawler.

She smiled, shaking her head. She had a nice smile. "Thanks for the interest, Ron. I just worked in offices. I was an art major and then I edged my way into office work. Boring! I did love going to punk and new wave concerts and clubs. In dangerous neighborhoods, although with girl friends or with guys. I like classical concerts, too, but the people aren't exciting–"

"Too normal? Too sedate?"

"Yes."

"Then you heard there were jobs in Japan?"

"Yes, but I knew I would have an easier time if I got some ESL/EFL training."

"CELTA?"

"No. TESOL."

"And how is it?"

"I like it when I visit people's homes…especially when they're in the countryside. The countryside here is very beautiful. And people are nice. They often feed me very good food. I also like it when students are personal with me. But I still miss New York night life…Not the working life." Her voice had become anxious.

"And Naoko?"

"She's almost a friend, when she isn't a boss. Have you met with her yet?"

"No, I haven't. Have you? As a model?"

"No, that will be soon. Tonight, it will be as her teacher. We'll talk about it then. She's supposed to show me her sketches."

"She's supposed to show me her sketches. I'm anxious to consult with her. We're going to talk about how to dress you up! The right clothes, colors, technique."

"And what are you thinking?"

"I wish that door down the aisle had had bright rays of color: yellow, orange, silver, off-set by black."

"Was I supposed to be a sun?"

"With the clothes I would have put on you? I don't know. Is that it?"

"What clothes?"

"Have you heard of Hanae Mori? A friend of mine loves her. I've been looking at the fashion books at Maru Zen bookstore. And there's a library that has such books. I also like Yohji Yamamoto, but that's it. I have a good pictorial memory, but I'd love to have Naoko's Polaroid camera."

"You're going to copy one of them?"

"No, I'll start with one of them and then vary it to my taste – just as I'll do with you. If someone who knows you sees the painting, you do want deniability, don't you?"

"I'll answer that when I see it. But for now, I'll trust you. And I'll trust Naoko…And I want to be there when you discuss your approaches to me."

"You want a lot! But not too much. I want you there, too. Marla, I'm enjoying this. But I'm not painting. Do you want to be painted today? Too late! You're being painted."

_*_

"Are you going to see Naoko, Ron?" asked Aoi.

"Yes, but not socially. I want to see what she's done with Marla. I also want to study her brush marks. She may teach me something."

Aoi was incredulous. "And pay you something."

"I don't think I interest her that way. Her shimei are normally younger. There's too much mind between us. A turn off. No money from her, I think. But that's not a promise, Aoi."

"You may take her in your arms anyway! Or she you. It wouldn't be good for a guest to complain to the owner that you turned her down. Anyway, she seizes the moment. She might deal with you the way she dealt with that manager the first night."

"Aoi, you remember! And know people so well!" I sighed.

"Those I've seen before! You know what I mean."

"Of course."

I have described Naoko as a beautiful 40, with piercing eyes. I was now so pierced, but rather than beautiful, I thought her nose, cheekbones and chin naught but handsome, still powerful. She might have misunderstood my queries concerning her artistry as simply a gambit. In any case with the eyes of a bird of prey, she made it her own, and we settled on a good price. Yes, it was fun.

Such rapacity – hers, I mean – can be a rush. The vagaries of style are almost everything. Instruction in the techniques of her painting would come – could I be present the next time she painted Marla.

She had already shown me what she had. Except for black and yellow, the colors were different. But she had retained the door except made most of it glass a bright silver and grey. I liked the green, too. More words here would not come easily; my first language is painting. Was Marla to be a sun? Well, at most, stars are similar.

_\*_

Our meeting was unexpected. Aoi and I were together upstairs in the art section at Maru Zen bookstore inspecting the wares. Looking up and back, I was startled at the sight of them. They were not looking at us, but surely, they had upon first entering. So many unseen would in their place have withdrawn.

We were dressed in the most casual street clothes, not so different from Aoi's usual studiously conventional dress, but not at all as they had seen me. Nevertheless, I turned to Aoi. "Marla and Naoko are here. Shall we meet them?"

"You shall have to, Ron! I can look at pictures."

"For only so long! How about just polite introductions and a quick departure?"

She nodded and after a moment we stood behind them. Marla was picking up a book I already knew. "Hello, Marla! I see you've got Sugimoto there. He lives not so far away, you know."

Marla appeared to genuinely start. "Oh, Ron! How are you? Oh, Sugimoto! Naoko pointed him out."

"Fine." Then turning to Naoko, who seemed startled not at all, "Hello, Naoko! My friend here is Aoi. We're leaving, but we thought we'd say Hello."

Naoko smiled cagily, "Aoi! I've heard about you. Do you model for Ron?" Aoi shook her head.

"We're firm friends," I said. "We can't talk for long. We've got an appointment. Aoi, this is Naoko. She's painting Marla here."

"Nice to meet you, Naoko. And you, too, Marla. Naoko, I can only wonder how your rendering of Marla compares to Ron's. Perhaps, I'll see it sometime. Good luck with it."

"Thank you, Aoi," said Marla. "You're very pretty, Aoi. Prettier than me. You should model."

"Thank you, Marla. You're very kind. Perhaps I'll think about it."

"Well, Aoi, our friends are waiting. Naoko, Marla, I'll be in touch. Good-bye for now."

-*-

As soon as we were on the first floor nearing the door, Aoi, as expected, exclaimed, "We need to talk!"

"We do."

"Shall we find a bench in Sakae?" referring to the square nearby in the heart of the city.

I nodded. "It's warm enough."

But the discussion began at once. "Ron, I need a change. A big change."

"Away from me?" I used to answer. Now I only nodded.

"Let's sit down first," she said.

"That was the plan."

"I want a child. Instead, I've had an abortion. But I still want your freedom. But to do what? I want nothing commercial in my relations with men. But what do I want then? I don't know, Ron! I think I need to get away."

"To leave me? You've always been free to. How could I ever have stopped you?" The reader can guess that this had all been said before. "A plan, Aoi? Where, at least, do you want to go?"

"To San Francisco? I could tend bar. My parents taught me. I'd only have to learn some new drinks. I could learn those from a book, probably."

Was I apprehensive? Jealous? I admit it.

And her? The intensity! Her timing! Not merely jealous of those women, but of lives not already hers!

"Well, you're thinking this. So, you'll continue. You know what I am. Now you'll seek to know what you are – who you are!"

"Yes, Ron. I'm leaving to see who I am without you – hopefully only to come back to you. I do love you, Ron. I always will."

That I doubted, but said, "I can say nothing more, Aoi. It will be you who does."

_*_

"Marla, are you still modeling for Naoko?" I had decided upon a change of scene. Odd how I had only once before visited a splendid park like Tokugawa-en. Why was my favorite Tsuruma Park? But never mind!

"Yes, and still without you on hand! What's happening, Ron? Are you on the outs with Naoko?"

"I've called. She doesn't seem interested. Nor have I seen her at the club."

"So, no conference on artistic technique?"

"We once had an exchange. I guess I didn't bring much to it. I was the only one with questions. Marla, do you think you know her?"

"No, how could I? She's opaque – more than you! I don't think she's very happy. Her marriage is probably a trap. But who knows what other people she has in her life! The husband probably doesn't know. Why should we?"

"Marla, do you like modeling for her?"

"For her. For anyone whose conversation is interesting. Posing by itself is boring. I'm too restless."

"So do you think you'll stay in Japan?"

"If I can keep going to people's homes. In Chiryu, for example, there's a couple; they're sculptors. The wife is one of my students at a place called Yahagibashi by Okazaki Castle. I've been to their house. They once had me come on Sunday morning for a sake brunch. That was after I told them about champagne brunches in America.

"Anyway, they live next to two kindergartens close together where in the morning I teach for 30 minutes each. They have me come very early on that day for breakfast. They also help me with any Japanese expressions I need. I have routines I do for the kids, using English for the nouns and the verbs, but the story lines have to be given in Japanese. I won't go on and on about it much as I want to. But I want more experiences like that. The trouble is that there's not much money in teaching at that level. I'll stay longer and think about it. I'll still go to host clubs if someone like Naoko will take me."

"I'll tell you if I hear of teaching jobs like that."

"Will you, Ron? Thank you."

I had the feeling, however, that I would not paint her again. She was part of an adventure that began and, I suspected, would end with Naoko's interest in me. I would of course give her any help I could if she called.

In truth, I could not long think of either Naoko or Marla without missing Sachiko.

And Aoi? Was she leaving not just Japan, but me? I had of course filled her head with stories about San Francisco, but there was more about her that I have said nothing about that made me think – ruefully, I admit – that San Francisco might be right for her.

# Aoi
# IN WONDERLAND

$C$onventionally, when a man wants a woman, he must risk or
suffer the intervention of certain types of other men: if not
rivals, then fathers, brothers, or pimps (as well as such concomitants
as ministers, priests, or vice officers.) But, until recently, my own walk
of life wholly attenuated these concerns. My wife, Aoi's father, could
be taken as a father either negligent or too grateful to see her married
despite her origins to a man of means. Only the most unsophisticated
husband could regard me, or be regarded as a rival; against this sort, I
was shielded by men like Aoi's father as well as by the very conditions
of work. What "man of substance," I thought, would brave the stigma
of being seen with Aoi?

But such security is uncomfortable, and I must surely have been
compensating when I agreed to agree with Aoi's plan to go alone to live

and work in San Francisco. But having filled her head with so many stories, how long could I have resisted her curiosity and quickening anxiety about her life with me?

How long had she taken to settle! For a time, she had no stable address! Her parents confirmed that she was all right. In her letters and calls, once so frequent, too many names – like rain, really – had glittered and pitter-pattered. Here I even wondered about such things as her liking for Playboy and the art of Louis Icart, or even our encounters on the street with especially beautiful women. Once when I had wondered gently aloud, she had wept, compelling me to recant.

Understand that I would have respected her choice. Too many women in clubs were ashamed of needing other women, and, as a courtesy, mind you, I made introductions. (For in truth, I at bottom dislike pimps, and took it badly when a man suggested even in jest that he be mine.) Be all this as it might, I now suspected it was someone unnamed.

"A captive wife makes one captive," I had always said, "and captivity is for the very young, the very old, and the infirm." Yes, I've been told that talk like mine is for a certain type much too young. Yet how suddenly can a beloved friend's farewell age one! And yes, how eerily can an absence slip into the length of a farewell! (So insidious is life!) What had I expected? Only that "things work themselves out," I recalled. I was throwing her to the world, or rather letting her throw herself, hoping that boomerang-like she might return, perhaps...what? wiser, more mature, with greater self-confidence and self-respect? Yes, more deeply than I could recall doing before, I acknowledged that she was lacking for me. Could any woman so satisfy me that I could not let her go so far away? I had to smile: "Let every man, woman, and flower be free!"

And with that refrain, I quelled every worry, every fear until finally after a month-and-a-half, I received the letter of almost a different woman. Grudgingly, I recalled she had once effused over me as she did this man she now described, this Kurt. Oh, an almost entrant at Juillard! (She was becoming quite an entrant herself, I thought.) They had met through a friend, a one-time friend of mine.

A girl friend, actually? I suppose so. I had been in love with her. She with me? Never mind!

Kurt? I had probably met him no more than twice at Bobby's apartment in San Francisco. My only lasting impression was that having his looks would have advanced my life's work – that part of it that accounts for most of my estate, shall we say.

But to return to Aoi. Her most salient comment, "Ron, I did something very naughty. You said that I should make a lot of memories over here (omoi de wo tsukuru) to enrich my life.

But let Aoi explain [with some untagged insertions by me; expressions and manners, as I think they must have been]: You told me that you only discovered me by degrees. You meant that you discovered my advantages only by degrees – my advantages over other women. Remember? You told me about some of these other women. I only remember her name, I think, because she is the only one of them you seemed to love. And, of course, she is the only one who still lives near San Francisco. [And, of course, Aoi had seen one particularly provocative painting of her.] I wanted to meet her. You said yourself I was going there only with the dreams you had given me. Of course, those were the dreams you seduced me with, seduced me into bed, seduced me into marriage, seduced me into the kind of unmarried friendship you really wanted. Well, I wanted to meet this woman, this Pulcherrima. I think it's an ugly name, but a man told me that it means beautiful. ("She's meeting some educated men. Now if she can meet one for whom it's not just a subtle arrivisme.") You said she lives with her husband in Tiburon. I went there alone.

I was unable to get her number from information; I thought it would probably not be in the Tiburon phone book either. But, please believe me, Ron, that I would not have been creep enough to approach her at her home. But I might have gone by just hoping to see the woman in one of your paintings.

Actually, when I finally boarded the ferry there, I did so mostly expecting to visit the town. But find her? Not likely, I realized. But I would try.

I decided that if she was worth meeting, she would like the places I like as long as as they were expensive [like her father's place – 10,000 yen just to sit and watch for an hour.] There is a place in Tiburon – not far from a lovely place right on the road where you can, if you're the sort of person I'm not – taste small mouthfuls of wine until you're drunk. So many of these silly people come in. I didn't stay inside to see them, but I stayed a long time outside just watching them come out. I wished at the time that you were there with me, but now I am glad you were not – I would have been too accepting of your explanations. You have said I should think about the people who come at those awful hours to my father's place. Well, of course, Ron. It's just that in another culture, it takes longer, a lot longer. People here are really different when you meet them than just in an American movie, aren't they?

So, I then walked into a place I shall never forget: How beautiful that place is, Ron! It isn't only that the bar opens onto a (What is it, Ron? A "terrace"?) Anyway, you can sit by the water. It's also the only place I've seen in America where older people and their children want to sing the same songs. Even songs I learned in English classes – not the stupid, boring ones like "Twinkle, Twinkle, Little Star," but "I've Been Working on the Railroad." For the wealthy, a paradise! (Jesus, Aoi, some of those women, if they were Japanese, could be found at your father's place!)

I was off to one side by myself and tried to remember the words of some songs. I talked with two elderly gentlemen and with the two sons of one of them. Finally, I went inside.

Then at the bar, I saw someone I thought might be your friend, Pulcherrima. I realized how crazy it was to approach anyone just for her resemblance to a woman in a painting! I think if I had not met so many strange and often not very good people in my parents' place, I would not have found the courage!

You joked once that if I ever saw any of your old girl friends, I should just tell them, "Ron says, 'Hello!'" I did. She was seated at the bar with a handsome man she said was her husband. After what you told me, I was suspicious. But he was. He introduced them as, "Mr. and Mrs. Herbert Johnston."

Aoi was never really to know her, so I'll comment here – and opine. Pulcherrima: Though apt, the name is so pretentious. But, then, I suppose that is just Americana. Someone in a bar once told me that farmers in Nebraska decided on classical Greek designs for the state capitol. Were they pretentious? No, the man told me, they needn't be the fount of their civilization to wish to join it.

Pulcherrima's father was not a well-educated man, just a post office functionary who, I think, was simply proud upon the Caesarian birth of his first daughter and, perhaps a little humiliated – or just amused – when a nurse countered with an explanation his laughter upon seeing the name on a list. (Or so Pulcherrima had related.) A chance apprehension of distant fathers in conversation or in a name, sometimes an American's only reflection on origins.

"Please do not call me Pulcherrima! Just Bobby."

"I'm sorry. Ron told me. I didn't think it would matter. I thought you wouldn't really be her."

"And how do you know me?"

"A painting of a very beautiful, exotic woman! With dark, golden hair." And with a nod to Mr. Johnston, "You're very lucky."

"Thank you. I know it," said Mr. Johnston, with a wary smile, beginning to relax.

"And you are?" queried Bobby.

"Aoi. I know Ron. I've never been his model, though. I like his painting."

Mr. Johnston extended his hand with a warm quizzical smile. As Aoi accepted it, he said, "I'm Herbert. Herb, if you like. What brings you to America, Aoi? I usually see Japanese in groups. Actually, here, not many people come alone."

"I'm just looking. I've heard a lot about San Francisco. And the Bay area. And now, three days a week, I study hairdressing. Hair dressers in Japan make a lot of money."

"Money's good, Aoi. A woman's got to have her own." Aoi nodded and thought him kind.

At that moment, Aoi was startled by a man behind her, "Bobby! Herb! Having fun?" Aoi turned, her mouth opening with a sigh at the sight of a tall, well-muscled man with Bobby's coloring and hair.

"Kurt, this is Aoi from Japan," said Herb.

"Hello, Aoi. I've been told Japan is full of beautiful women."

Aoi shook her head. "But thank you."

"Aoi, you've come to the right place. Tiburon is full of beautiful men – like my brother here, Kurt."

"If you'd said something like that to Ron about the beautiful women here, he would have said something like, 'Is it? I'll try not to get them mixed up.'"

"Debonair in his way. Do you know that word, Aoi?" asked Bobby with a hesitant smile.

"Cary Grant."

"Yes! Cary Grant. Very good, Aoi."

For the interested, Herb was the latest of a whole succession of bankers; Bobby, no doubt, the latest in a succession of trophy wives, a type I love in all but marriage. She had begun, however, as a model to finance her B.A. in art with a minor in business management, later managing an art gallery.

"Aoi, I play piano at certain clubs and with a couple of bands in the Bay area. I tried business, but music is what I do."

"I like music. Japanese, British and American pop, some jazz."

"Aoi, do you want to sit down somewhere and talk? Or do you want to just continue wandering around?"

"Go on, Aoi," said Bobby, "Keep him company. He gets lonely fast and this one?" (pointing to Herb) "He's mine." Herb commented with a comic shrug and smile.

As they walked away, Kurt asked, "Do you want to go for a drive?"

"No, walking is fine. Take me around Tiburon, Kurt. So many beautiful homes and gardens! And the Bay!"

"Aoi, I don't live here. I live in San Francisco. I only come here to visit my sister…And the pleasures of girl watching are limited. I don't have the money these babes require. The young ones, I mean. The older ones have their own."

"Just like in Japan. I understand. Well, I'm staying in San Francisco – at a boarding house for now."

"So how about walking around a bit, then as the sun sets, I drive you back to San Francisco. You don't know me, but I'm a gentleman, Aoi."

"Walk me to the ferry. I'll give you my phone number at the boarding house. We can talk more."

Talk they did; Aoi made him persist. But, eventually, when they did meet, Aoi asked what she had forborne from asking over the phone (lest she have to answer in turn), "Why did you ask me out on a date, tonight? Don't you have a girl friend? You're very handsome. As beautiful as your sister. You must have a girl friend," said Aoi when they were seated on the terrace of Da Flora in North Beach.

"Yeah, I know a lot of women. But nobody steady. But you're interesting. Mysterious…"

"Really? Why?" (I can see that skeptical smile.)

"What you know! Who you know! …I like Louis Icart. A man only needs to like style and a woman's body to like Icart. It's not great art…"

"Yes, that's what Ron says. He doesn't care… But he says he's getting tired of it…He's getting older and more serious, he says."

"Languid joys are not for him?" Aoi's eyes must have told him.

"Sorry. 'Languid' means...Well, he doesn't wish to be care-free any longer...When he was young, did he just gaze lazily hour upon hour at beautiful women and then go paint some? That's being languid."

"Yes!" Aoi started, "How did you know? Oh, Bobby told you...Yes, I forgot."

"No, no. Bobby didn't tell me. But I've always thought Icart must have...Anyone would say that. Anyway, deeper things interest Ron now. How old is he anyway?"

"Now –" The waitress came up.

Kurt looked up with a smile, "She'll order for both of us."

"Kurt. Most Japanese aren't that Japanese," she replied with an excited smile, referring, I believe, to their eagerness to please a guest. She ordered, but she saw he still wanted his answer. "He'll be thirty-eight in April – just in five weeks!"

"Older. You must think I'm a child."

"That's what Americans think of me...I'm twenty-seven. My birthday was two months ago."

"Okay. I am a child. Twenty-four."

"But you're innocent...Ron –" She stopped.

Kurt was shaking with his laughter. "I'm not innocent," he said.

"Ron is less so... and if a stranger had said that of him, he would not have laughed as you did."

"So-o-o," he said with a grin that the waitress thought was for her, "He has a lot of women, too!"

"He has more than he needs." (This probably with a wild, nervous grin.) The waitress hurriedly set down the dishes, perfunctorily accepting Kurt's perfunctory Thank You as well as Aoi's unnatural one (She had ceased reserving her thanks in the Japanese fashion for the moment of payment.)

"Well, he doesn't need Bobby either, obviously, so did you really come just out of curiosity?"

Aoi's mouth firmed (much as it did when she was relating this), "He needs me for a friend. And he looks after me."

"Good friendship," Kurt said demurely, "Please tell me, Aoi, what kind of places you and he liked to go to together."

Aoi probably became a little wistful, for I know her heart toward me, but remembering herself, she answered fluently, "Art museums. Ron loves art. Temples. He doesn't like Japanese cities, except at night, but we both love the countryside. You don't know how beautiful it is! We go – went to quiet places. He loves to paint. But then –"

"But he doesn't love you. Is that why you are here?" Kurt asked gently.

"I looked up at him," Aoi told me later, almost laughing, because he was so wrong, and said, "'I'm here because he...because in a way he told me I should be...for a while.'"

Kurt sipped his wine, then smiling intently into her eyes, asked, "So you're free to meet other men...like today."

"Yes. Aren't you free to meet other women?" She smiled back. "If not, it is not I who am stopping you. So, who is? Tell me."

Ignoring the question, he asked, "So, Aoi...That's a lovely name. You told me you like music. Have you gone to concerts here yet?"

"No. They're expensive."

"Discos?"

"No, in Japanese discos a woman who goes alone stays alone. The men aren't supposed to come up to you the way they do here."

"Really? They don't? Well. But doesn't Ron take you?"

"No!" she said sharply, "He used to like rock clubs in San Francisco and Los Angeles...New Wave. But he likes classical and international."

"And you...do you go with him to classical concerts? Piano music?"

"Yes. Mozart. Chopin, and Liszt, and Keith Jarret and Oscar Petersen...," she nodded happily.

"Good. If you can make it tomorrow, I'm performing at O_____ Church on Van Ness. Don't feel you have to come by yourself," he said with a gentle smile, handing her two tickets.

"One is good," she said, nodding with an excited smile, "I'll come."

-*-

"Such beautiful skin...even without make up!" cooed Bobby on Aoi's next visit with Kurt - this to her home. She had found Aoi sprawled by the pool her face to one side. Turning slightly, Aoi smiled a Thank You. "You keep Kurt's hours, some of his friends... Not their drugs...or not much...Some pot probably...I'm guessing... You look good!"

Aoi purred with her smile. "You modeled for Ron, didn't you?"

"No."

"A lie," thought Aoi, "a stupid one, too; she's forgotten the painting I saw," until she remembered my sometimes inserting into a painting someone observed unawares.

"No? Why not?" she continued, "Doesn't he like you? I thought you and he were good friends? Or were you his girl friend? Didn't Ron let his girl friends model for him?"

"Depends on what you call a girl friend."

After a pause, Aoi asked, "Did you ever love him?"

"Depends on what you call love." Aoi thought she understood, and only much later doubted it.

"Do you mean you might not have loved him, or that you just feel that what you felt might not be what I would call love?"

"That's too deep, too difficult. And not worth it, Aoi. Not to me. I don't know him anymore."

"Ineffable? That's a word I like…Do you think Ron ever loved you?"

"Yes, I think so now. Before I thought his… I thought it was just sex he wanted."

"Why do you now think he loved you?"

"I stayed in his mind…"

"How do you know?"

"I don't. He's ineffable. Not really, but I like that word, too. I don't have to explain or know anything – but I'll try…It's the way you're acting." Aoi did not persist. Bobby did. "In the painting you recognized me by, what was in it?"

Had Aoi paused longer, she might have resisted. "You're with two other women, young and beautiful – like you? Your seated in a chair with your face and eyes poised cutely –"

"Coyly?" Bobby offered tensely.

Aoi grinned quizzically before saying, "Coyly? Coyly toward a photograph."

"What's in the photograph?" Bobby interjected.

"It was never meant to be clear. It's indistinct… Anyway, one other woman is seated in an armchair with her left leg raised on its broad arms and her other leg on a foot rest pointed toward the front of the picture –"

"Corner foreground?" Aoi shrugged, and was silent.

"Continue," Bobby ordered. "…Please continue."

"Anyway, the woman is looking absently beyond the photograph. The other woman is also on the carpet beside you but with her head on your knees and she is looking beyond the painter." Aoi was elated with Bobby's sudden passive expression. "All of you were wearing bathing suits."

"I don't remember that one," said Bobby dryly. "Tell me more about it." Aoi detailed the chair and the room. Bobby eventually replied that she still could not remember it, then after a perfunctory remark about her memory, excused herself. How that painting had delighted Aoi! She now feared that she had made an end of the adventure.

_*_

The party was unusual in that Bobby and Herbert had told Kurt he might bring certain of his late-night friends. But he brought only Aoi. I suspect this occasioned a change in plans – Bobby's – for they were soon in her bedroom. She abruptly followed and sat down before Aoi. "Aoi, I want to ask you something, and I want an answer." Aoi turned to Kurt and found him non-committal. "I want to know why you are here. Do you intend to drop little pieces of my past with Ron or his friends, so that people can pick them up and take them to Herbert? Is that what you want to do? Are you an enemy?"

Aoi thought a moment and with some bemusement turned to Kurt, "Kurt, are you really taking things back to Herbert?"

"No, he's not!" shouted Bobby, "but if you're playing with me about what paintings you recognized me in, it means you really want something to be known!"

"I just smiled," Aoi later explained, "She is so lovely! I'm jealous! Ron, how could you have ever noticed me? Anyway, then I said, 'I just came to see what you were like...Your brother was unexpected, but if you're that thrilling for Ron, I'm happy for him – envious really.' I was afraid to ask her if she wanted me to leave.'"

But Bobby persisted, "What are you to Ron? You're an ex-girl friend, aren't you? Not an ex-wife? What is he doing over there?"

Aoi sighed and shook her head, "I'm not an ex-wife or girl friend. I'm a friend."

"But what does he do? Does he work in a bar?"

Aoi reached for a pen lying on a desk and wrote my number on the cover of a magazine. "Go ahead! Call him and ask anything you want! There's a seventeen hour difference, but tomorrow morning may be good."

Then addressing Kurt, "How can I get back at this hour?"

Kurt sighed, open-mouthed, then said, "My sister and her husband don't really know each other well, but you're Japanese. How well do husbands and wives know each other there? I mean at first. Don't people keep quiet a lot – about a lot? Herbert is concerned with appearances, too!"

Aoi slapped her knee, guffawing uncharacteristically, then smiling, perhaps impudently, at Bobby, said, "'Respectability is mostly appearances.' Isn't that what Ron told you, Bobby? You must always go for the same kind of man...But this one's got money! And a nice place! I'll be –"

"You bitch!" shouted Bobby, rising to her feet. "He wouldn't touch you! He wants an older woman with money." Kurt rose, but said nothing. "Yes, he likes them. He really does like them. Besides, they're all he can afford...Or were. And he doesn't have to settle on just one! –" (I've always been appalled by the meanness of younger women, even my own, whenever compelled to acknowledge the charms of their elders.) "And they're easy to meet – those well-preserved women who come to buy paintings from him...," then with a malicious grin, "Your friend, Ron, was probably a gigolo!"

"Bobby!" Kurt interjected, taking her shoulder.

Aoi suppressed a smirk – she enjoyed relating all this – and replied, "If he was, I would know...You were one woman without much money whom he did love...He told me."

At Kurt's insistence, Bobby sat down again. Regaining her composure, she chirped, "He loves any beautiful young thing without clothes."

"Yes, that was his type, but no more, he says. He wants someone more serious, more sympathetic, more understanding. Not a party girl always about town –"

"Not you then," Bobby mocked.

Aoi frowned, then her shoulders fell, and she put her head in her hands and wept.

Bobby stared, probably in wonder.

"You wanted to be that wife, Aoi?" Kurt asked, rushing to take her in her arms.

Bobby began nodding, and said, "You are that woman, aren't you, Aoi? Think about it, Kurt! She drinks very little. She doesn't dope even when everyone else does. She came to the city alone, and did this thing by herself…You're his girl in some way, aren't you, Aoi?"

"Hai!" said Aoi, holding up her flushed head to Bobby. Then repossessing herself, she said, "I'm Kurt's girl."

"Not his only one, Dear. But you know that, Kurt tells me."

"I know it. He's my boy friend of convenience!"

"You are convenient, too, Dear. You don't make him wear condoms, he tells me. Pills don't prevent disease. Make them all wear condoms! I just don't know how to make my husband do it. But never mind, Aoi," she said, again rising to her feet, this time clearly to leave. "Listen, Aoi, a shared silence can be a good place to begin a friendship. Meanwhile, you two help yourselves to the food. After this conversation, I'm famished." Then with a coy smile as she closed the door after her, she called out, "I'd get you a drink, but I don't want to cripple friendship."

Thereafter, Aoi did not require condoms of Kurt. Nevertheless, they were together for only a month longer. Kurt had not proven himself very strong. But then, perhaps it was just that the mystery was so fragile, even if I never did receive Bobby's call.

_*_

There was nothing unusual about the clinic Aoi entered: a receptionist behind a window with other personnel behind her, women with or without men with or without children behaving as they might, not all of the women visibly pregnant. She took a seat and flipped impatiently through magazines available on a low table, the sort one usually sees concerning pregnancy or health.

She does remember one of them: Family Digest and a picture of a baby inside of a womb. She turned away to observe a white girl in her teens her condition apparent, biting her thumbnail and spitting it out on the floor. Aoi's chills and sighs were not at all for herself. She still wonders if she should have ventured a conversation.

She looked farther about and saw a woman in her 20s haggard, probably ill.

Looking again at the picture, she felt her tummy. She sighed. She would have to tell Kurt. An abortion he would demand and she refuse – to her satisfaction. Her last pregnancy and my demand for an abortion haunted her.

I remember, "Aoi, how can I be a father to anybody? What kind of upbringing can I give to this child. We'll have to keep what I do a secret – what your parents do! At least until he or she is older! Otherwise, school will make him or her feel like a freak! No, I don't want the responsibility! I can't give what I must!" She began to cry. That proud woman rose and ran out. I followed. So did her parents.

"What will marriage to such a man be like, Aoi?" had asked her mother.

"Freedom and respectability," she replied. "He's a university educated painter and English teacher! He knows I'm the daughter of host club owners and wants me. Nobody else wants me when they find that out! Until then, they know that we own restaurants. We make sure that even their managers don't know what else we own. I can be open with Ron. I don't know what kind of father."

Aoi's father was unexpectedly conscionable…Had he actually lived long enough to learn that money really isn't quite enough? He nodded, "Hai. Hai. Hai. True. My unhappy daughter; we have made you this way."

"He won't accept the child?" exclaimed her mother. "What kind of man does that? You're his wife!"

"It figures," her father said. "We shouldn't be surprised. But, Aoi, how can you stand to live? I don't want a dead daughter. You must be strong, but how this strong?"

It was I who was deadly: So many times, she imagined my insistence and her refusal of an abortion. And thoughts of suicide, the child never born. That thought she practically spit out of her head, hating the world and probably me. Then she thought of begging me to let her remain formally my wife so that she could live in San Francisco on public assistance if it was available before getting bar work that might pay for day care. She had never enquired about it.

How long she walked! I had had to caution her that especially after dark San Francisco streets were not safe. In Japan, she had only to be apprehensive while crossing at intersections lest some hentai (pervert) step out of his car to accost her.

# Sachiko's BirthdayParty

I t was an occasion for remembering my discontents with Japanese space. In two days, I would celebrate with Sachiko her fiftieth birthday. With a seamless grace would I receive her! Still, what is grace, but a granting of coveted space? The walls themselves had proven stingy enough when I had hung the paintings she had stood for. I had still to decide which of those to oust should she bring certain of my old gifts she had (supposedly) never dared to show even her closest friends: among them, a series depicting her former life. (I recall how nervously she had brought her family photo albums here for me to study.) I could recall other things: the hours of purposive motionlessness in sessions over two years, through which, her earlier vexatious chatter and nervous distress had gradually yielded to a deeper patience and introspection; the occasions when she had broken down, helplessly awash in tears, confiding in me, seemingly with everything she had, when we had then gone for a walk (or, more rarely, to bed); and, most wonderfully for conversation, the mornings following a rare night together when we would patiently, even lazily, prepare a breakfast we had read about, sometimes while snacking a little on fruit salad and orange juice or white wine. Yet this space, so evocative of memory, was surely sumptuous enough only for me.

She needed space for friends, too. Where would I seat them? But no, who would they be? No one, as I have said, with whom she could share her house could she share her time with me. No, not one of those she listed as friends (except for me, introducing me as "an artist and English teacher"), and, who would list themselves as her friends, would she or could she invite to this party. Who, then, might I fill it with, or failing that, where might I take her to thrill her into a forgetful bliss?

More immediately, how might I thwart, on this occasion, any sequel to that doleful probing she had brought us both to only a week-and-a-half ago? "You're a good friend, Ronald," she said, tapping with a finger a cooling cup of tea beside her with the pensive calm of a strong woman in distress, "You're probably my best friend. To what other person am I able to speak as I do to you? And I've tried to find others like you. How many of these 'wild Americans' are as staid and conservative as any Japanese? Though, to be sure, you're not the only one who is interesting and charming...Still— (Yes, ending with a sigh), "Where is there another Ron-san?"

"Such an expansive declaration of love on my account! You must mean it...I'm sorry I'm not more satisfactory in bed –"

"You've gotten better...Why shouldn't you have? Money's not everything to you, Ronald. That's why I can love you in the way that I do...Why do you still meet women in the clubs?" I gave a tired sigh, and she waved the question aside. She looked down, then up at me, "Ronald, I've asked this before, too, but I want to ask you now.

45

Do you need love? Do you need...Does your life need to be about something?" She forbore elaboration.

"The question is twofold, isn't it? Love and meaning. Two parts of the real question: Why do I live this way? Are they not, Sachiko?"

Sachiko nodded, and I continued, "To begin with, I need love. Our friendship – it's more than a romance, isn't it? Just as I would have it. Our friendship – now four years old! – should prove it, even if the circumstances of my marriage, and, I suppose, those of the rest of my life appear to bely it. I've said this before, but the longer we're together, the greater reason you have to believe it..." She nodded to this, and again I spoke, "Now as for meaning. I paint, and if I must resign myself to mediocrity, painting is still something I love. You know this. That's also what keeps you here. It's the other thing. I whore. I whore for money, and I whore for adventure. I think you could say that in this latter case, I whore to annihilate meaning. If I leave off whoring, it's not because I have enough money. Rather, it's because the circumstances have crystallized into one kind or another of ugliness that the money can't redeem."

"For example?" She was smiling tartly now.

"Perhaps merely physical or personal. I've told you all this before. There are a lot of people who repel me out there. That also goes for many host club owners. [Not all of them, though. Aoi's parents aren't the only ones I've taken to...] I've yet to meet a yakuza that I've been able to like for very long. They did use to stimulate my curiosity, though...The answer, as you've seen, is simply to flee...All the same, Sachiko, you can say whatever you want, but I still think I have more freedom and independence than working people in your country or in mine...Besides, I won't continue doing it. My body has to weaken, and it is; but my mind is also outgrowing it. More and more, it seems all too much the same...Meanwhile, I invest, and make deals, and teach

46

English. Money, money, money...Money for security and freedom, for a future, and for the idle time that some idiots use to inspire them to suicide. Isn't that what you're really asking about, Sachiko?"

She slowly lifted the cup of lukewarm tea, and drank almost half of it. "Yes, I've wondered about it. You're not alcoholic yet, either."

"Neither are you, Sachiko. Why are we having this conversation? Do you feel it coming on?"

"Maybe I do, or something else like it. When I was raising my two boys, and thought myself a cherished wife, I knew why I was alive everyday. I would never have thought to ask why."

"Paradise never lasts, Sachiko. That's why we become adults. Can I get you a glass of wine, Dear?"

"Yes, Ronald, give me something white. And while you're at it, distract me by telling me about Naoko and Marla."

My recollection was dissolving into a collage of fantasies, when the phone rang. "Moshi, moshi. Oh, Aoi, it's you," I said in English, "Where are you?"

"In San Francisco. I need to come home and talk to you about something...Okay?"

I noted the waiver in her voice, but only said, "Sure, but when?"

"I'm leaving tomorrow morning. I've just decided it...I'll explain it when I come...get back."

"Sure, my dear, do you have many things? Should I pick you up? I am busy right now...very busy, but I can pick you up..."

"No, I can get back all right. I'm not going to stay here long, I think...Well, maybe I am. I don't know yet...It's complicated. I'll explain when I get back."

"Okay, Aoi, I'll be expecting you. Listen, Sachiko will be here the evening of the 7th. That's in two days. Call me, as soon as you get here, all right? I want to pick you up!...Okay?"

"Okay, thank you," she said, uncertainly, and then abruptly hung up. I hate to drive on Japan's small roads, but I also take care of my own, and, besides, I wanted to hear before I met Sachiko again what could be so important.

"That was Aoi, Sachiko! She's coming in a day or so. Is that all right? We don't necessarily have to change our plans."

"No, but now I need even more to be distracted. You were about to do so."

"Yes, you beauty! I shall," I thought.

"Naoko? How is it that we could have art in common and still not get on? Marla studied art, but is not a painter, but we could be almost friends. It's nice to talk with another American – one like her. She loves art and likes to talk about it. But she is so full of curiosity! She's quite young and still deciding what to do with her life. She's thinking about returning to America and becoming a children's teacher! Ours is a service economy and she hates offices! She seems to have found herself here – as a teacher!

"She concedes that the day may come when she's too old for the nightlife. But until then, a double life for her!"

Sachiko was aglow. "I'm so pleasantly distracted! Do let me meet this Marla! I want to hear all about it!"

"You shall, Dear!" And she would.

-*-

Even when she was living here, Aoi usually complemented Sachiko's visits with a discreet absence. This evening, however, she elected to stay in her room. She had money to go anywhere she liked, but there could be no better refuge, I'm sure, than that private quiet. In any case, she had no friends she could frequent the town with, pouring out her thoughts, especially her present thoughts. Not all of them were unhappy. She was expecting a child in seven-and-a-half months.

It was only I, who made her unhappy. No, I had replied with the cliche usually given in movies or whatever, "No, I will not lend my name to another man's child." At any rate, I had never intended parenthood. Indeed, we had had one child aborted. Our words this time were bitter, but brief. I said nothing unexpected, and she quickly withdrew to her room. She heartily agreed with my insistence on the party. I agreed that this was her home, too, and, that, in any case, she should not be alone in her mood. I would bring her dinner.

I did not tell Sachiko everything, but I knew she would not require an explanation. If I am ever wise, it is in my choice of friends. Sachiko assisted with the last of the dinner preparations. Then we moved most of it into the living room, placing it all on a dark, low, flat table. I smothered one of the pale, red lamps, so bright was the moon through the bay windows. Surely, a September moon in Japan looms more hugely and sensuously than an Occidental moon, indeed, a Genji moon. Ours was not a Genji repast. So Sachiko would have it of late. Neither was it unmindful of the occasion. Sushi, sukiyaki, and sea food and fruit salads with tea and wine. Only I would drink sake. The moon drifted aloof from the clouds.

"Would Scheherazade please you?" I asked, lifting an LP partially from the case. "Scheherazade? Oh, if you're in that mood, perhaps we should just go straight to bed – Oh, I'm so slow. Forgive me, Ron...

you do have a lot on your mind...Do you think Aoi would care for Scheherazade?" Such passionate smoothness! Could she really have gone to bed with me with Aoi in the next room? Had she really once been the conventional matron she recollected?

Aoi had eaten only salad for lunch. When I asked what were her doctor's recommendations, she answered, "Bring some of what you're having – without the wine. Tea and milk, please." I knocked to ask for confirmation through the door, but she opened it wide, and stood facing me without a word. By this did she intend to announce her acceptance of whatever Sachiko and I would offer? Could she only know how little we had spoken about her! I would have liked then to be able to invite her to dine with us. What was this now fulsome longing holding my tongue? I eyed her still merely plump form with jealousy and dismay. Still, I knew that she was at last for me a woman. With both hands, was she not seizing for herself a difficult, if not degraded condition?

At last, I found my head. "What will you have?" I asked with affected laconism.

"What I told you this afternoon. How is your girl friend?"

"As well as she's ever been. How are you?"

"Fine, thank you," she said, mimicking many a past English lesson, "And you?" Suddenly, her gaze flicked past me. I turned around.

A relaxed Sachiko beamed at me, but especially at Aoi. "Good. Please join us. No one should be miserable on my birthday. And I will be, if you stay in your room like this. Come and join us. Please. Ron will go out and get some milk and cookies, if you like. Won't you, Ron?"

"We have it on hand," I said, ecstatic with her boldness and generosity. "But perhaps I can get to another shop I know and find some pate...What do you think, Aoi? Would your last doctor approve?" I looked over at Sachiko, and said, "I'll explain in a minute."

"Yes, pate and crackers will be fine. Buy some more milk. And some chocolate for it, too. I still have to get used to the sugar they put in it in Japan, " Aoi replied.

I looked once more at Sachiko and said as matter-of-factly as I could, "Aoi is expecting. Don't worry. Everything's under control."

Sachiko's mouth opened and her head dropped. Then after a pensive look, she nodded. Ah, me! Not the best time to leave them to get acquainted! I could not be called a coward, I reflected, as I went out the door – but fool would do pretty well. Did I not intend sabotage? Of course, I did, but only with the thought, "We shall have done with this tension, or we shall have done with one another!" I thought I would take longer than necessary, and check their mood with a telephone call. (How I should have liked to eavesdrop!) I found the crackers, but not the pate. Sachiko's voice had exuded only a controlled cordiality. But – ah, me – in those circumstances, well and good. And, of course, I did not return to warmth. At any rate, I reported on the shopping, and Aoi went into the kitchen to make herself some chocolate milk. Sachiko stood and eyed me with odd detachment. I thought I knew why. The extremity of Aoi's position had doubtless made her bold with confidences, dropped, I was sure, as challenges. The damned themselves do a lot of damning.

Pretending not to notice, I asked in a low voice, "So, Sachiko, is it possible that you'll make a new friend? On your birthday? Do you like Aoi?"

"Yes," she said with a tense sigh, "I do." The pause was brief, but leaden. Then she added, "What about you? Do you only like her? Is she only welcome as a convenience?"

"She's not always a convenience, nor has she ever been," I countered.

"She's bearing another man's child. No one will blame you for divorcing her. The lover ought to have taken responsibility for the baby," she said with an emphatic nod. I was a little shocked. I had always thought her better natured. Only much later would I entertain the notion that she had only roughened to test my heart. How many Japanese have flattered my prowess only to elicit boasts that would confirm their fear that I was a scoundrel?

Sachiko's eyebrows were still raised when I slowly replied, "She never seriously suggested that I accept the child as my own. It was just an opening gambit."

"So what can she do?" Sachiko snapped, "Live on her own? Go back to her parents?...I've heard that women do this in San Francisco...It must be quite a place...Anyway, it's not done here. She's crazy! What did she think she was doing?"

Before she could answer, Aoi returned, and Sachiko sat back in silence. Aoi stayed only to collect some food on a tray, to thank us, then went to her room. Reassuring me with a quick smile, Sachiko called after her, "Aoi, I will call you—soon!"

"Yes, soon, Sachiko," Aoi called back.

I quashed my apprehension with the thought, "Good. What will be will be." Surely, it could not have been coincidence that I now remembered those of my old portraits she had brought. How like an Aeneas wandering from the ruins of a fallen city she had appeared, though without mandate from on high – or low. Nor had I thought to presume upon this neglected office. No, I had been all too happy to entice her into this benighted life. Still, with a Dido's solicitude, I had hoped with my paintings to condole her for the disaster that was my boon. (And to make her thankful for it?)

The paintings were already removed from their boxes and mounted when Aoi reentered the room. I was not as apprehensive as one would expect. I had already told her about them. I had explained to her that while Sachiko's former life was not my life, I was fascinated by it, and wished to show my respect and sympathy. Aoi knew them at once and only Sachiko's burning, bright eyes dared reply. Not for the first time I thought that if I had been one of her employees, she could have as quickly made me happily supine.

"Aoi, would you like to see a wonderful series about the married life by someone who has never seriously undertaken it? By someone who would flatter me by portraying it as I once thought of it. You ought to see them." She pointed to a portrayal of herself lifting with loving arms her first infant son. "The colors are mostly red and brown, like the earth, I think."

At that moment, I thought, "How wonderfully bold! When will this child I married ever be able to match her?" Then I was ashamed: Hadn't she already? Wasn't I too impressed with Sachiko? She gambled with elan, but with my stake. Still, would a conservative tact have sufficed? How, then, can I fault her for what followed? I admit that I have often fostered much in Aoi that is unJapanese. Still, every decisive step was taken by her.

"Does this son...What is his name?"

"Yasamasa."

"Does this picture charm Yasamasa as it does you?"

53

I answered for her, "She doesn't know – but it might. Only for some few seconds scattered over these four or three-and-a-half years have I ever seen her face as radiant as I try to make it here...I often imagine he would say the same..." I wished to take Sachiko's shoulders reassuringly, but also possessively in my hands.

But I had to allow Aoi her moment. I awaited a retort, but her eyes fell away from me, as if deep into herself. She, then, walked limply across the room, taking Sachiko's seat. Shrugging her shoulders, she finally said, "Do you ever think that when you're in bed with her?"

Sachiko's mouth and eyes opened with something that I thought would become a tired resignation to go to war. I took her arms with a resignation that became warm relief to tell her and Aoi both, "Yes, Sachiko, there are moments when I am with you that I do think things like that. And" (with a wave of the hand)" of course, when I'm painting them. Those are the moments that prompt people to marriage...IN the best of cases, I mean. But..."

"But what," asked Aoi in sobs.

"Yes," Sachiko echoed in a whisper.

Not for the first time, I thought, "Tonight, I shall lose them both."

In place of "But what about the rest of them?" I said, "But what kind of father would I have been?"

Sachiko warmed, and Aoi sighed, if without hope, at least probably without blaming me. Women! Say what you like, in so many ways, they're all the same. As I expected, Sachiko broke their long silence first. "Aoi, will I still be able to meet with you later?"

I smiled tiredly. "Sachiko, this meeting sounds pretty important, and our party does seem to be over...And I do confess that I could use a drink...I'll be just down the street." Sachiko sighed.

But Aoi stopped me at the door. "Ron, you should stay. If you don't, you should know what was said. Sachiko, we can still meet later, if you think it is necessary. I want to settle this now, please. I came back to Japan to settle things. But I didn't..." She awaited our replies.

Sachiko answered my look, "Yes, Ron, please stay...You have a drink here. We all can..."

"Aoi, I'll get you some milk," I insisted.

"Yes, some milk. Forgive me, Aoi, I forgot myself," Sachiko added.

When we were at last seated around the tables, I said, "You were about to say something, weren't you, Sachiko? Please, we know each other, and why we're together, don't we, Sachiko? Please, trust me. You won't surprise me." Before she could answer, I passed a tray of sashimi over to Aoi. "Please. This may last past the child's bedtime. He or she will need to be strong. Eat. Excuse me, Sachiko."

"That's all right, Ron...Yes, I know why we're together...," she said, slowly gesticulating, "But why, Aoi, did you marry this man if you wanted a life like the one I had...?" Then anxiously looking back at me, she added, "Ron never gave himself out as that kind of man, and I never wanted him for that...So I don't understand."

Aoi shot back, "No, he never gave himself out as that kind of man! He never painted such pictures for me! He never spoke well about the married life! He never spoke well about romance...and passion! Why? He just wanted a friendship. A friendship in –"

"'A friendship in freedom' yes, that's what he offered to me. I wanted it – with him. It's less than what I once had, but you know that. I told him that. He said, 'Too few know the happiness of being No. 2. No. 1 has too much to live up to.'"

Aoi brought her hand down sharply on the table, reflexively pushing away the sashimi. "Oh, you're quoting him. A lot of people do. He is so funny!"

Sachiko turned to me. "Family life is just some far away place you want to visit, not some actual thing you want to take up?"

"What a question, Sachiko! We've known each other for almost four years. And you ask? Family life is a foreign country I like to hear about...Yes, sometimes I get jealous. Perhaps, I'm always a little jealous..." I looked out at the table at so much food not being eaten, and reached for the sake. I took it in a beer glass.

"Yes, we've discussed this before."

"But only a little. Too many of these people covet – well, not my life, but the freedom that goes with it."

"Yes!" Aoi hissed. Sachiko eyed her fixedly.

I decided that I might as well speak. Turning to Sachiko, I said, "Yes! That was my appeal for Aoi..."

"You were married?"

"No!" Aoi shouted, "He's my only husband. He means I just didn't have his advantages!"

"As you know, Aoi's parents are host club owners. Among my former employers. Her marital chances weren't very good."

"Maybe, but excuse me, Aoi," Sachiko said turning with a respectful tone to her, " but that doesn't sound like an environment to inspire much respect for marriage in a young girl...I'm sorry. But you did marry at what? 22...23?"

"23."

Sachiko was silent.

Aoi continued, "Ron is handsome, isn't he? He's smart. He has a university degree. He paints. He's interesting, isn't he?" (Sachiko nodded.) "And he's free! He can do anything! Wherever he goes, he's as respectable as he wants to be. He has money..."

"Nobody needs to know from where," interjected Sachiko with a grin.

"Now, I saw him being like a god, flying high over every cloud, every storm. He's like a submarine. No storm can sink him. Of course, he's always running, but it's not important to him. One place is like another for him."

"As long as it's in Japan. My way of life is legal here in Japan," I said.

"Yes," Sachiko said, "like an old American, you found your opportunity by going westward...all the way to Japan! You said that once."

"Yes," I replied with a broad, excited smile, "to Japan! Where men are men and women are women! Where I, a man, can live by doing precisely as I please! And you, dear wife, I let seek your chance as Japanese usually do by escaping eastward – to San Francisco! Where women remain women only if they want to!" Only Sachiko and I hazarded a grin.

Crumpling under this humor, Aoi said at last, "Whether it's a boy or a girl, I want to! I want to be a woman! I studied hairdressing in America – one class, but it's a little different in Japan...I have money, Ron, but not enough. Oh, never mind. I'll go to my parents. And if they won't help me out, I'll..."

"And I'll go look for an English teaching company to sponsor me," I thought. I had never applied for permanent residence. I would now, I knew, but said nothing.

Sachiko got up. "This is between you two. I'm sorry. I was wrong to come here tonight. But, then, I wouldn't have, if you, Ron, had told me Aoi was expecting. Please pardon Ron and me, Aoi. I really have forgotten myself! Aoi, sometime soon, let's get acquainted…if by any chance, that would make you feel better. I know it will make me feel better."

Aoi brightened in surprise. "Yes, Sachiko…We'll meet sometime soon."

"I will lose them both tonight," I thought once more. But why this eagerness of Aoi's? Not the beauty of a fifty-year old – or of a personality of splendid power? Suddenly, I knew what I wanted to say. "Sachiko, please, I still need a long walk and maybe a drink alone afterwards. You can stay with Aoi. I know you may not believe it, but she wants it. I know she wants it. I want that walk…alone. Please! At least, leave after me! You can talk now while you still know what you want to say."

Sachiko gave me a look of protest, and asked Aoi if it was all right. Aoi said Yes, and I left. When I returned, not only Sachiko, but Aoi, too, was gone. At first, I was not truly aghast.

"Thank you, Sachiko, whichever of us you meant to help," I mused.

Then I realized that each might have left on her own. It was too late to call Aoi's parents (It was not a club night, but she was with them when I called the next morning.) I insisted that she return.

"Is Sachiko staying in your life?" she asked.

"Yes, I think so. To be honest, I plan to call her next. How about in your life? Is she staying in your life? Or was that just two ladies making a display of their best manners? If so, I'm impressed, but disappointed."

"I don't know yet. Do you think she and I could really be friends?"

"I don't know yet either. Last night, you seemed to think so. By the way, did you leave together or separately last night?"

"Together. She dropped me off. We didn't say anything. She did say she would call me. I think she likes me. She also said you won't always want her in your life on account of her age."

"I won't always want to go to bed with her, if that's what she means. But I may surprise her. Usually, the problem with women older than she is whether I like them or not. I accept the decay of the human body, including my own. And that's more to the point. I'm already too old for this life. Why don't you think about that on your way home? Our home! Do you want me to pick you up?"

She hesitated, then replied, "I want to stay a couple of days. I need to think. I'm hardly out of bed. But thank you for calling. I know you care in some way. You're just strange. Well, you're always interesting. Maybe you always will be. I'll call, okay?"

"Okay, I'll see you. Bye-bye."

Words, words, words. Now to have some with Sachiko. Sachiko was at work, very sleepy. "This is not the way a business woman should be," she said.

"When will I see you again?" I asked. "Soon, I hope."

"Oh, when will you have time? You're very busy, aren't you?"

"Not for two days, unless Aoi wants to come back sooner. I have to meet someone for an English lesson tonight. Tomorrow evening?"

"Ron, I think I should try to meet with Aoi first. Let me do that, then call you. Maybe we can meet next week." At the end of the week, the two had met twice, but neither was ready to see me.

"How kind! How prudent!" I thought, "Neither is inclined to strive against the other, and it would be useless for them to do so. If you can't beat 'em, join 'em. What my women have is sense!"

My absence in the nearly three weeks that followed must have served them well, for the next time, the two of them appeared together, even appearing assured (But, then, only Aoi was taking a risk.)

Before relating this meeting, I must relate another, this one with Sachiko alone that led to it, or, rather to the meeting with Aoi alone that directly led to it. She, Sachiko, insisted, that I meet her where I seldom have – her home, and with pretexts so transparent that I agreed without further protest.

I should have been apprehensive at such an invitation from most of the women I knew – older and married – but Sachiko is also my best friend. Still, I was not really used to meeting her son, Yasamasa, much less at the door. Yet, as always, he was entirely cordial. When I asked, he said he would soon graduate from Nanzen University, and yes, his brother, Hiro, was already enjoying married life, though still a student. (The sort of duplicity my life often requires, you understand, though I truly like the fellow. The moralistic reader should perhaps pick up another's memoir.) At any rate, he was then quick to take me and a pitcher of iced oolong tea with glasses to his mother where I had never met her before – in her garden.

So, for the first time, I was seeing her with her second brood she sometimes spoke of: her cabbages. With her hair bound in a navy blue scarf, kneeled over in old blue jeans and tennis shoes, she might have been anyone's curvacious and classically featured middle-aged mother. She stood up to greet me as we approached. "Well, what do you think of them?" she asked when pleasantries had been exchanged, "Remember, they're your rivals, even if I have to be jealous for them. So, answer carefully."

"I can tell they're yours. Just as beautiful," I said to set alight her new moon smile. I was reminded of the phone call from the host club where four years earlier we had failed as client, and whatever it is I am in these things. There I had recommended a part to play; now, I sensed, she was writing an act. She poured me a glass, and, taking none for herself – I saw a large empty glass on a rock – she knelt once more. I remained standing.

"I asked you this before, but it's only natural to ask this again: What do you plan to do with her?" she finally asked, rather studiously scratching the ground with her odd-looking tool.

"What you can already surmise, I think. I will let her bring the child into our lives as my own. We live by lies anyway, and by now, I should have made it clear that I think they can make life interesting. Anyway, the next move is hers. That's us. What about you, Sachiko? I need a wiser, more mature presence in my life, and Aoi knows it. She has always known it."

"Of course. One woman isn't enough for any real man," she said sarcastically.

"No more, apparently, than one man is for the kind of women I select for my life," I countered. "She genuinely wanted this life of freedom, and as for my money...Well, what man isn't taken for his money?"

"What did you take her for? What are you taking her for now? I know she hasn't been home to keep you from having to clean and cook. And she hasn't born you children! It couldn't have been just for the spouse's visa. So why?"

I sighed with a smile from a deep place. She spoke with anger – the anger of her love? But I answered as it pleased me, "Haven't you wondered why she didn't stay in San Francisco to find a man who would take her? There are so many who would. She chose the child's father not just for the obvious pleasures, but also on the basis of eugenics. Without the slightest conceit, I can say that I am the only man for her! I suppose you could say that she loved me as a child loves a bird soaring in the sky, only she couldn't become a bird herself. She's more a boomerang. My boomerang. Even her parents' boomerang. Even I need something like that, and probably need it more as I get older."

"And, I, you will be needing less," she said with tense finality.

"Quite likely, Sachiko, though, with Aoi back, I continue to be (mildly) dismayed that I prefer your maturity. But it's not only your family that has kept me from wanting to live with you. I know I'm not the man for you. Not that I think you seriously prefer the man you're married to...If you tell me that, I shall laugh at you! No, but you seriously prefer the man you married! I can only live with a woman for whom my life – in part, at least – is home."

"Don't say, 'in part,' Ron Dear, for you are that much to me, and when Yasamasa leaves home, you will be that much more... And you may still need an elderly, clothed subject for a painting."

"I shall have to meet with Aoi alone as I am meeting with you." Only then was it awkward for me to stand, and picking up Sachiko's large glass on the rock ("Ii – good!," she said, taking it and filling it half-way), I sat down. I soon quaffed most of the tea remaining to me. Sachiko watched me finish, then filled it.

"Please," she said. "Please show the same eagerness to talk everything over with Aoi. I agree: she is more important, especially now. But take her, take her over me, only if you have what she now wants!" In my apartment, the passion would have found consummation. I rose, emptied the glass (turned down her offer of the toilet), and promised to call soon.

_*_

Aoi shocked me. "You don't understand! I do understand! I wanted a child! I used to want you for love; now, I would only take you for your support. Your money! I think I could still take your friendship if it is worth anything more than that. And I doubt it!" We were seated on a bench on the grounds of Astuta Jingu (one of the largest Shinto shrines in Japan, a beautiful, often eerily empty place for any couple to date or fight without attracting the attention of anyone who matters). There, as I have said, Aoi shocked me, even dismayed me —but only for a moment.

Then I started with delight. "My darling, Aoi, yours is an attitude I can work with! Hasn't it always been so? Yes, please reenter my life, our life! But this time, we shall be together more often. I shall be at home more often. I've told Sachiko – and she must have told you – that I'm really too old for this. And, besides, my investments are paying off more and more. But let's not plan anything definite, except...except that...no more women at the house! Not even Sachiko!"

Her mouth opened, "There are others? I thought they were just business."

I shrugged, "There have been two others this past year – just briefly, just briefly. They haven't been back, and I haven't invited any more. No, no more women at the house..."

"Do you really mean you will say Good-bye to Sachiko?" asked Aoi, laughing in disbelief.

Raising both my hands such as I rarely did, I replied, "Well, I didn't say that! But I do want to say that I don't want any men of yours at this house –"

"I never did!" she shouted.

"I know! I know, but I don't want it to start! Take them some place else!"

"Okay, okay," she said with a grin, "But I really just want to raise my kid in a quiet environment. I wasn't really planning to have a lot of boy friends."

"And I wasn't really planning to give my name to any more of their kids. (My face was one suspended laugh.) But don't commit yourself on anything else. Remember, what's that saying? It was stolen by the Beatles. 'Real life is what happens while making plans.' And remember what I say, 'Real life always costs money, so always plan to make plenty!' Well, anyway, no more women at the house..."

"Yes, my Master!" she said, her face still aglow, "Do you think it will work?"

"Do you think it or anyone else – particularly in this country – will work for you any better?"

"No, Ronald, no one that I've actually met. Though there are strange stories like that about Americans, and Japanese, too."

"Yes, I've heard them, too. More of them than you have, I think. It's my business to know. It's inspiring to think how people make it in life! A cause for hope, don't you think?"

"It'll have to be, Ron-san."

"A mature woman at last," I thought. If I were a mature man, one could say, I wouldn't have to pretend to need to meet them together like that, but how many things in my life – or their own, since meeting me – ever needed to happen? But, then, if I were a mature man, shouldn't I be faithful to our common spirit?

I knew Aoi always had coffee with lunch, but I spent several hours in Hongo, looking for a large coffee house with an especially varied menu that upon request could include warm milk. I would have preferred, of course, the sort of place I normally associate with the making and confirmation of deals, but this was to be for a kind of deal less nocturnal. I reserved a place in the corner for 2:00 p.m. when the place would be almost empty (I hoped.). I told them that the occasion was a family gathering. Even for a 2:00 p.m. appointment, reservations even at a place that does not require reservations can be expensive – particularly if one wants the surrounding tables as well. (Nagoya is a large city, the sixth largest port city in the world, I'm told, but gossip in Japan can be like that of a small town.) I won't describe the splendors of M_____. Why should I, since I'm only giving you an initial? Besides, the nicest places are only for night people. What isn't?

Some would-be ex-night people met for what? As a reform exercise? Quite. Children, particularly the unborn, are insistent. (If someone says he or she hates or loves them, remember – the little fire-crackers brought it on themselves.) Even as Sachiko sat down, I thought her despondent. Aoi gushed with devil-may-care pleasantries – from a contented resignation, I hoped. I thought some important things should be said before we ordered. "Sachiko," I began, "I want to tell you this: I love you and I want you to be in my life for as long as...as I can see forward. I also love Aoi, but in a different way. You two have been talking with each other these past...what? Three weeks?"

Both demurred, then with a nod from Sachiko, Aoi smiled and spoke: "Please, neither of you, worry about things. Sachiko, just have Ron call at the house before you come over, or call yourself. We do have to cover ourselves with whoever may be over. Don't we?"

Sachiko and I nodded. "And Sachiko," she said, turning only to me, "knows that I don't blame her for the way our marriage has worked. It's that life of yours – your work – that I want you to get out of. Just teach English and paint. Sachiko and I can be your models. Of course, you can have others as long as you don't take up with them. Or at least, move your painting out of our apartment. I want some place that is mine and the child's..." She nodded to Sachiko and me with a smile. Sachiko and I exchanged brief smiling glances.

Then Sachiko took an unexpected tact, "What about the child? You expect to remain in the house, Ron? For your art, probably, but for whom?..."

"For all of you," I said. What else could I have said? I never intended to be a father.

"May I pursue the question – since I have less to lose by asking?"

I nodded.

"Children like to keep the same friends. They like to keep the same parents. Absent fathers they don't like, but they can tolerate it if things are always the same. Later self-confidence comes from the experience of certainty at a young age. You have this odd constancy with two women in your life. It's one reason for liking you, for trusting you. So far, we're the only thing I haven't seen you running from. Can you do it for a child? I'm just wondering."

I smiled wryly at Aoi, "Would you like me to answer?"

"Yes, Ron, I'm curious. I want to see what you'll say. Of course, it's not as important as what you'll do."

"What I can tell you is this. I like children – so far, other people's children. I will not be cold or indifferent to one in my own house. I will let you decide how she is to be brought up. I will help you. I don't know how much, but I will help you...But I want to ask you. What kind of person do you want this American-Japanese child to be? Japanese schools won't help her understand or appreciate either of us. Her racial mix won't help much either, especially when she's young. Do you want me to give her – or him, I'm sorry (Yes, at this, the women were charmed; the raising of a daughter in these conditions intrigued me more, I admit.) Do you want me to give him or her advice? You know what my advice is like. It's for people who have already ceased being children, or who want to. Let me put it another way, a child starts life the way he starts riding a bicycle – with training wheels. This means that he or she is given certainties to live by for the sake of helping him or her approach life with a self-confidence that is not justified. Later maturity consists in part of comprehending in the practice of life the strengths and weaknesses largely of what he or she has been told earlier. An oversimplified way of putting it, perhaps, but probably true enough – generally speaking. What do you say to that? As far as this child's upbringing, just what do you want to get away from, Aoi? Do you think the child should grow up to be ashamed of your parents, or of us? That's how you grew up, as I recall."

"Yes, Ron, that is how I grew up; only you could have made me regard it as an advantage. Thank you, Ronald. I guess that's why I still love you in a way. Who else could have done that? Yes, Ron, but don't advise him to work at host clubs! Yes, that part of my parents' and your life, I do want him to feel, well, two ways about – more against than for – not like you, like me, like Sachiko..."

"Why not wholly against? Why these half-measures? Look what prostitution has done for me?"

"It's like you've always said, Ron. Everyone wants your freedom!"

"Yes, Ron, and your magnificent courage to go your own way!" Sachiko said. "Give the child that! Aoi and I discussed that. She or he will never be like the others. Probably not happy, but with a great chance to be interesting to a great many, maybe a leader, or an artist. Who knows?"

Aoi, bright-eyed, nodded, and smiled.

"Such foolish talk!" I reflected. But they probably knew that. I knew that this was a conversation that would continue for all of our lives, even if we shouldn't always remain together. When had I been as fatalistic as I was probably to become? I thereupon decided upon a frivolous expression of a very serious hope. "Aoi, somebody told me that a great French writer I should read said that every great fortune begins with a crime. And since, as you know, I always like to say, 'Real life –'"

"Ron, please, we both know, 'Real life is what happens while making plans, but real life always costs money, so plan to make plenty'." Sachiko can be quite impatient.

"As I was about to say with fewer words – but I'll make it still shorter, 'Every great fortune begins with a crime.' With that in mind, I hope for all our sakes, that I've done my work well." The women laughed.

"And even if you haven't, and you should come to regret all this, you can remember what you told me, 'Paradise never lasts, Sachiko, that's why we become adults.' And she nodded affirmatively.

Aoi pulled Sachiko over for a rough hug and a kiss, then as roughly kissed me on the mouth. Then seizing my gaze wildly with her own, she said, "And don't forget it!"

I nodded, and after reflecting a moment, I stood and signaled to the waiter. "The family matter is settled. Do you have any champagne?" The waiter demurred.

"Not in this place, not at this hour at any rate," I said aloud to myself in English. "Any wine?"

"Hai."

"Then two bottles of red? White?" I asked, turning to the women, "Just to lighten up, before we order."

"White!" said both, but Aoi added, "To lighten up? Not to forget?"

"No, never to forget," then with a (probably) mock grimace, "There's not even enough red wine in stock for that."

Sachiko shook her head, smiling, but Aoi's eyes opened wide with an odd smile.

"What Aoi?"

"You've forgotten. Me, too. White for another day. I'm expecting. Tea and milk, please."